AF472022

Christmas Rages On

J.E. Steinman

Lulu Press

United States

Christmas Rages On

Published by
Lulu Press
www.lulu.com

This is a work of fiction. Names, characters, places, and incidents either are the product of the author's imagination or are used fictitiously. Any resemblance to actual persons, living or dead, events, or locales is entirely coincidental

ISBN- 978-1-257-096176-6

Printed in the United States of America

First Edition January 2011

A hundred times a day I remind myself that my inner and outer life are based on the labors of other men, living and dead, and that I must exert myself in order to give in the same measure as I have received and am still receiving.

—Albert Einstein

Christmas Rages On

Chapter 1

Kristen walked slowly into the small white room, quiet, as not to draw the attention of the young children that sat at a small table coloring. She stood just inside the door, watched them. It was easy to see the heaviness in her young heart through her sad eyes. After taking a deep breath, Kristen stepped to the table, and stood behind a little boy with blonde hair. His clothes were a bit large for him, causing him to keep pushing the sleeves of his shirt up out of his way as he colored the picture he had drawn. A picture that made Kristen's heart feel even heavier inside her chest.

"That's very good, Toby." Kristen commented with a forced smile, her eyes pooling as she fought back the tears. Toby was only ten years old, but his drawing ability surpassed his age, surpassed Kristen's entirely. She leaned over Toby's shoulder, touched her hand to the paper next to the green leafed tree and brightly colored flowers around the base. Next to the tree, kneeling down to smell the flowers was a woman with long yellow hair, and at her side, holding her roughly crayoned hand was a little yellow haired boy. The rest of the paper was filled with green grass, blue sky, and a bright yellow sun that Toby was still filling in, making it larger and larger.

Kristen glanced around at the other pictures that the other children had created. None was as clear, or defined as Toby's, but there meanings were just as clear. They were all of things that the children missed from their past, normal lives. Lives that were a daily event until a few months before, their lives prior to the Rage Virus being unleashed into the world, and humanity's fall, from it's sharp teeth and claws.

"It's my Momma…" Toby said softly, his voice small, sad, and without a touch of hope. "Wasn't she pretty?"

Kristen stared down into his sad eyes as he looked up at her with an expressionless face. She wanted to take him into her arms, hug him, let him know that everything was going to be okay, but she couldn't. She didn't know if it would ever be okay again. She suddenly had an overwhelming urge to run from the room, run down the hall to her room, lock the door, and cry.

"Miss Kristen, are you okay?" Toby asked when her only response to him was tears starting to stream over her soft cheeks. Toby twisted his small body in his chair, and wrapped his arms around her waist, burying his face into her shoulder. "Don't cry Miss Kristen… you're just as pretty as Momma was."

Kristen gently combed her fingers through the boys

hair and hugged him back. She let her hand glide down over his flushed cheek as she pulled away from him. She wiped her eyes and gave Toby a comforting smile. The same beautiful smile that had comforted him since the day the soldiers brought him to sector five.

"I can draw a picture of you too, would that make you feel better?" Toby asked with a smile of his own.

"I would like that very much."

"I want to draw you too!" Karen shout from the seat on Kristen's right.

"Me too!" Added Jason and Alice in unison on the other side of the table.

Kristen stood straight and gave them all a grin. "That's wonderful, you all get started and I will check back on you in a little while." She walked back over to the door, looked back at the four children already starting their new projects. "You guys behave, okay."

"We will!" They all called out, not looking up from their work.

Kristen knew all too well how the children felt, each of them had lost a parent, some both, as well as siblings. They were all so young to have felt such loss, and had no idea how to deal with it. She did the best she could to comfort them, help them through their mourning, but it was difficult to help them deal with what she had been unable to cope with herself. And the fact that they were all now stuck a hundred feet under ground, and had not see the sun in months wasn't helping at all. She couldn't help but wonder what kind of life they were living, if that is what it could be called. Just as the children, Kristen longed for her normal life, one that is lived under the sky, not tons of dirt and concrete. Something had to be done, and she was going to do it, normal was a must, and she was going to bring some back to them all. The problem was she just didn't know how.

Back in her room, Kristen's eyes once again filled with tears as she laid on her small cot, a loose photo in her hand. The photo was one of her standing between her mother and step-father, taken in front of the lake, shortly after her mother had married Alex. Kristen remembered that day as if it were yesterday. Even through her tears, she could not help but smile. That was one of the best days in her life, the day they became a family. Kristen could almost feel the heat of the sun on her skin, smell the water and fresh air, and she could without any doubt feel the love surround her again. But when the door to her room opened, and Carmen limped across the tiny space to set next to her, Kristen was quickly reminded that it was just a memory, and that her mother and Alex were both gone forever.

"You okay Kris?" Carmen asked her best friend with true and visibly concern. She gently stroked Kristen's side, her hand came to a rest on Kristen's hip.

"I was for a minute." Kristen purred, showing Carmen the photo, a weak smile formed on her lips.

Carmen returned her friend's smile as she took the photo into her own hand. "You were so lucky to have them." She said, her own tears starting to flow. "They loved you so much."

"We were luck to have them Carmen, both of us. If it wasn't for them, for Alex, we wouldn't be here now." Kristen sat up next to her friend, hugged her, and they both cried. Neither of them said a word, but both of them remembered the last day they seen Alex. The day Alex sacrificed his life to save theirs, just as Kristen's mother had given up her life to save Kristen's. They both sat silent as the images of Alex running off, leading the mob of infected away from them, giving them a chance to escape to safety. They hugged each other tight as both reached the point that Alex vanished from their view, across an empty field and into the woods, barely visible beyond the fast closing mob that had no other intention but to rip him apart.

They had not seen Alex die, and Kristen was glad for that much. Her young heart could not have taken seeing him tore apart limb by limb by the twenty or so Freaks that chased him down. She only heard the final shot of his gun echo through the trees. Her mind envisioned what might have happened, even though she did not want it to, she had just already seen too much death, and how so many people had died at the hands and teeth of the Freaks.

Freaks, was a name given to the people that had been infected by the Rage Virus, by the soldiers that now protected them at sector 5, and had now become an everyday term to all of them. Kristen didn't really care for the name, but after hearing it used for months on end it had just become part of her vocabulary.

"So you want to make life in here more normal for the kids, but how?" Carman questioned, handing the photo back to Kristen.

"I don't know… I wish mom and Alex was here, they would know what to do.

"Yeah, they always seemed to make the best out of

everything, just like when we were at Dr. Klaus' lab." Carmen seemed to drift away for a second, into memory. "But they're not here, it's just us."

"Wait… I know someone that might be able to help."

"Who?"

"Sherry."

"She's not here either, remember? She stayed at the prison to help set up sector three."

"But we can talk to her on the radio… come on!" Kristen exclaimed, jumping to her feet. She grabbed hold of her friend's hand and drug her out of the room.

The two girls made their way through the long hallways until they reached the control room. They popped inside and was quickly met by Private Denton, as he stopped them immediately.

"Where do you two think you are going?" Max Denton asked, holding out a hand. "You know you are not to be in here."

"Max, I need to talk to Sherry at sector 3." Kristen answered quickly, so quickly the words nearly ran together.

"I'm afraid that is not possible." Stated Major Harrison. He spun around to face them in his chair at the large control panel.

"Why? It will only take a minute, I just need to ask her something."

"Kristen you can't speak to her, or anyone for that matter."

"But…"

"Let me finish." Major Bill Harrison stood up from

his chair, towering over the girls even though he was still six feet away from them. He lowered his head a bit, keeping his eye contact with the girls. “We didn’t want to scare anyone so we have kept it to ourselves, military personnel only.” He drew in a deep breath. “But I guess the time has come for everyone to know, hard to keep secrets when we are locked in a place so small and close.”

“What is it Major, what secret?” Carmen asked, squeezing Kristen’s hand, knowing the news wasn’t going to be good.

“We have lost contact with sector 3.”

“What does that mean?” Kristen asked, fearing the answer.

“We aren’t sure, could just be that the towers are down, or—”

“Or what?”

“The sector as been compromised.”

“You mean over taken, everyone is dead or infected!”

“Like I said Kristen we don’t really know. The last transmission from sector 3 stated that everything was good, but that was awhile ago.”

“How long is awhile?”

“Almost a month now.”

“It’s been a month and you still don’t know anything? What about the other sectors? Have they heard anything?”

“Well we haven’t had contact with them either.”

“What!”

“You see the power grid has been failing for some time, and we think that is the problem.”

"A month and you haven't sent anyone to find out what's going on?" Suddenly Kristen was feeling that same sense of dread that she had when Alex said he was going to lead the Freaks off so they could make it to safety. That was one feeling that she never wanted to feel again, but here it was, creeping up through her body like the infection itself, consuming her an inch at a time.

"We did, but we haven't heard from them either. We have completely locked down the upper level for that reason, to conserve power and keep you all safe."

"I want to go up, see out side. Maybe help is out there waiting for us, they just can't get in."

"That is very unlikely Carmen." Max said, stepping to the Major's side.

Carmen had said it, Kristen was feeling it. She had to see outside again. She had not felt so closed in as she did in that moment, knowing that the upper level, the only level that was above ground was locked off. "Yeah, but the people you sent out could be up there, out there waiting for us to help them. If the radio is not working, how would you know?"

"We run a video surveillance three time a day, there has been nothing but Freak activity up there." Major Harrison stated, stepping toward the girls.

"I want to see for myself." Kristen shouted, staring the major down. "Besides three times a day leaves a lot of time for them to not be seen, Major. You should be monitoring the area constantly."

"We don't have the power to do that anymore, we are running off of generators now, but fine see for yourself if you have to." Major Harrison turned on the monitors behind him.

"No, I want to see for myself, up there." Kristen needed to see outside, through windows where she could feel the sun's warmth on her skin, not on some black and white screen. The idea was far past what she wanted, it was what she needed. They had been down underground for so long that she had lost track of time, dates… She didn't even know what month it was.

"Absolutely not, that is out of the question."

"Why? Have the freaks breached the building?"

"No, it's secure, but—"

"Then why?"

"Movement will draw them back to us, we don't know how much more punishment the windows can withstand. If they make it inside the upper level we will be trap down here, no way to forge for supplies if we need to, and we are going to need to. We will be needing fuel for the generators soon."

"The windows are made of six inch thick glass. I don't see them breaking through." Kristen stated quickly, and to his surprise.

"How do you know that?" Max asked.

"We've been here awhile, not much to do but read."

"You read the specs of the building?" The Major questioned.

"My Step-father taught me well."

"Except for respecting authority apparently." Major Harrison snapped, turning his back on her.

"No Sir., I have respect for authority, more than most, but he taught me to stand up for myself, for others when the need is there, and the need is here. You are wrong for keeping us locked down here, we are not your prisoners, but your charges."

"That is true, Miss. And it is my job to keep you all safe the best way that I can, and for now this is it." Major Harrison sat back down at the control table, flipped the monitors off, and took a drink of his coffee. " And just so that you know, there is a storm coming in. Yet another reason to stay below. The temperature is falling by the hour, already down to twelve degrees outside, and thirty one inside the upper levels. To heat the area would use far too much power."

"Major," Kristen suddenly changed her tone, her voice was soft, sweet, and a bit alluring. "What month is it? I've lost track being down here."

Bill Harrison hesitated before answering, staring into the eyes of the two pretty young women that he had to keep from harm. He knew that Kristen was planning to do something to help the younger children, make them feel more at home within this concrete tomb, and tomb was exactly the way it felt to him. He thought about the consequences of telling them, weighed out the possibilities, and finally decided that it was for the best. Maybe Kristen would focus her attention back on the children, and off of the upper levels. "It's December, the tenth to be exact."

"December…" Kristen whispered back, her eyes fixed on her best friend, and then a smile formed on her lips and her eyes lit up for the first time since there escape from the barn. "Christmas… It's Christmas, that's it, that's what we can do for the kids."

Kristen took Carmen by the arm, spun around and

pulled her friend out of the control room, into the bleak hallway. She stood silent for a few minutes, leaning against the cold concrete wall. "They have to have decorations here somewhere, it's a government building."

"What decorations? What are you talking about?"

"Christmas, Carmen. We are going to bring Christmas to the kids. What's more normal than Christmas?"

"Your right! What a great idea, but how do we find the decorations? This place is huge, they could be anywhere… including the upper level."

"Sergeant King, that's how." Kristen started to walk down the hall, bringing Carmen with her, arm in arm. "He was stationed here before the outbreak. He should know where they kept the decorations. Come on he should be down at the cafeteria now.

Once they found Sergeant King, and after some deliberation, he decided that Kristen had a good idea. A little holiday spirit could go a long way, and not just with the kids. After he had finished preparing dinner, Steve King walked the girls around and gathered up as many decorations as the three of them could carry. After dinner had been served, and the kids were off to bed, Kristen and Carmen went to work, starting in the recreation room.

It was midnight by the time Kristen slipped into her cot, tired and drained, but she was pleased with what had been accomplished, and knew that the kids were going to love it. She had found a few packs of photos in the boxes that were of the building decorated for Christmas over the years. She loved the giant tree and star made of lights that stood high above the building. That was the photo she stared at as she drifted off to sleep, wondering if it was possible to light it up again. Steve King had told her that the lights never came down, that they were still strung high above the roof of the building, that they just fired them up every year. The thought of seeing that tree and star shinning high in the night sky gave her a warm feeling inside, a sense of hope she had not felt since she lost Alex. Kristen held on to that feeling as her dreams took over her reality.

Chapter 2

The howling cries of the infected filled the cold, dark air behind them. The actual temperature didn't mean anything anymore, their blood pumped so fast, so much adrenaline flowed through their veins, that their temperatures ran hot, and sweat slicked their flesh as they ran through the thick snow.

"Go, go!" The man out front shouted, rounding his arm, and pointing toward a storefront two hundred feet ahead of him. "Don't stop, keep moving, we're almost there."

Five people passed by him, pressing their way through the knee-deep fluff as fast as they could move. A blood thirsty howl sliced through the cold, burning their ears, and striking fear, pushing them to move even faster.

"Their getting closer!" A woman shouted as she passed by the man leading them and stopped just passed him, looking back. "Their too fast..."

"No they're not, just keep going." He shouted, ducking down beside a tall drift, taking aim through the snow filled air behind them. All that could be seen was white, white on white. Then there it was, a darker, gray figure moving fast through the white that had covered the world.

It really was moving fast, much faster then they were, and as it closed in on them it was joined by two more figures floating in the white behind the first, then another and another. The man ducked behind the tall drift, popped the clip from the rifle, glanced at it, then popped it back in.

"Shit... only four rounds left." He said to no one but himself. He knelt there, watched as the others neared the vacant store. "Well better make these count."

He swung out to the side of the drift, took his aim at the first figure moving at him fast, faster than any human could move through the weather they were in. He squeezed the trigger, and the muted pop of the riffle surrounded him, and turned the others attention back to him briefly. Before the echo in his ears stopped, the front running figure dropped into the snow and disappeared in an instant. He fire two more times, two more dropped, but the figures were quickly replaced by new ones.

The man turned and ran after the others, the figures closing in on him quickly. For a brief moment he thought he had waited to long to retreat, but with the door to safety only ten feet ahead of him, his worry started to fade, prematurely.

A woman, and a younger girl stood in the doorway,

encouraging him, cheering him. The only way to tell the two people's sex was their pretty faces, since they wore huge coats, and layers of pants to keep the cold at bay.

Five feet away, they yelled, and cheered, he ran as hard as he could. A loud howl filled his ears, a howl that seemed way too close. Two feet to go, he reached out to them with one hand, the rifle in the other. Two more steps, and bam! Something hit him from the side hard and fast. He went sailing to the ground, dropping into the foot deep snow. The thing that had hit him, turned on him, crouched down low, like a two legged lion ready to leap. It swayed side to side, measuring him up, readying itself to attack again.

The man rolled onto his hands and knees, faced the beast, and struggled to regain the breath it had forced out of his lungs. He reached to his back, retrieved a large knife. The rifle had been tossed when he was hit, it didn't matter to him really, it would have been mostly useless at such close range anyway, but he wished he had a handgun, he will have to get too close with a knife, and getting close to those *things* was not on his to do list. Not that he had a choice now.

"Watch out!" The woman yelled from the entrance to the store, half hanging outside the door. She looked as if she were about to run out to his aid, but the younger woman was holding her back, and struggling to do so.

The man twisted onto his back, rolling back onto his feet as the thing lunged at him. His blade slicing a thin line in the thing's exposed flesh of it's belly. The thing screamed as it landed and spun, still on the attack. It lunged again, it's hand swinging for the man's heart, it's teeth aimed at his throat. This time the man leaped into the air seconds before the thing made contact. His leg collided with the thing's hip, rolling him over the once man's back. The man's knife plunged into the thing's side as he started to roll, his empty hands reached around the thing's neck, arms locking, twisting the thing's neck as he rolled over it's back. Snap!

This time the thing stayed down, dead at last. But before the man could even think about moving toward the door, and safety, two more flew out of the wall of white behind him, blood-stained teeth bared, ready to taste his warm flesh.

The man spun, but they took him down just as they came into his view. Down into the deep snow the three of them disappeared with a howl.

"Alex!" Kristen screamed, setting straight up in bed. Tears filled her eyes, her chest heaved, as her heart pounded inside of it. Her eyes quickly darted around the dark room, lost to where she was, soaking in her surroundings until they became familiar to her again. "Alex…" She sighed, consumed by a great sense of dread. Kristen pulled her knees to her chest, wrapped her arms around herself, and cried with her face buried into her knees.

Suddenly the lights came on in her room, and Carmen ran in to her side. "What happen Kris?" She asked her best friend, embracing her.

Kristen leaned into her and cried harder. Engrossed in her loss of Alex once again as if it had just happened. "Alex…" She whispered again, this time into Carmen's ear, somehow Carmen felt her friend's pain as if it where her own, and in a way it was.

"I miss him too, Kris."

"I loved him so much… why, why did he have to —"

"Don't do that to yourself Kris." Carmen comforted her friend, pulling her tighter, and they both cried. "What brought all this back again, Kris?"

"I don't know… I was dreaming about some people running through the snow, here in the city. A man was leading them, and he reminded me so much of Alex. The way he moved, the way he was so protective of them."

"It was just a dream though, Kris."

"It just seemed so real…" Kristen drew in a deep breath. "It was like I was right out there with them, I could even feel the cold. I woke up with goose-bumps."

"Okay, that's a little weird, but it was still just a dream."

"Yeah, just a dream… but it was nice to have him back, even if just for a second."

"I'm sure it was. Can you imagine what it would be like if Alex was here, right now? Things would be so different with him running things."

"What makes you think he would be running this place?"

"Oh come on, you know Alex, he wouldn't stand for the way that prick Harrison runs this place, Major or not."

"You might be right, Carmen. Alex would not like the way things are done around here, and I'm sure he would find a way to make things right."

"Yep, just like someone else I know."

"What? Oh, I get it…"

"That is probably what stirred the dream, Kris, you taking over his role in making things better. Alex may have only been your step-father, but you sure are taking after him."

"I never thought of that, I do don't I?"

"Alex and your mom… God help that major once you really get started."

"Thanks Carmen, I feel much better now." Kristen gave her friend a loving hug, and Carmen excused herself and headed back to her room next door. But alone in her room, Kristen still felt a sense of urgency and dread, that something was coming, something that would change everything for them. She just wasn't sure if it was going to be for the better.

Again Kristen dreamed, this time the man had Alex's face, and he had survived the attack and was leading the small group carefully through the city, block by block under the cover of the blizzard. As her dream came to an end they had reached the northern edge of the city, and were following a bright and shining star high in the sky. They were almost there when the winds died and the snow stopped falling. Leaving them exposed in the center of the street, with freaks on both sides. They started to run, run for the star, the freaks gaining ground on them quickly, snatching a man from the back of the line.

That slowed them a bit, distracting a portion of the freaks as they tore the man apart with their hands and teeth, turning the deep snow red.

Kristen again woke screaming, with the name Alex on her lips, and embedded on her mind. "Could it be, could he still be alive." She asked herself, then remembered that day, the day Alex led the freaks away, allowing her escape. There were hundreds of them chasing after him, his only protection a single pistol. She felt it in her gut, as much as she did not want to, that Alex was dead.

Chapter 3

Over the next few days Kristen tried to put her dream behind her, blocking it out by staying busy. She and Carmen worked hard and vigilant at transforming the underground shelter into a holiday retreat. They hung garland, and set up Christmas Trees until there were no more trees to erect. By the time it was Christmas Eve, they had a tree in nearly every room. The recreation area looked more like the north pole than the dreary and drab entertainment hub that it was. The kids were all excited about Santa coming and leaving them presents.

Kristen's plan seemed to be working, not only were the children's spirits rising, but so were those of the soldiers, and other survivors. Morale was at an all time high, in their little tomb. The problem came when her joyful experiment started pulling too much juice. It didn't take long for Major Harrison to step in and put his foot down.

"You don't understand girls, all of these lights are burning up our electricity. They have to be shut off." Harrison ordered, his normal stern grimace on his weathered face.

"But the kids—" Kristen tried to explain, but Major Harrison would have none of it. Nothing else mattered other than the power they were using up. Power he wanted to keep stored for when the grid went completely down.

"No buts… they will be turned off, and now!" The Major demanded, firing a look at Sergeant King. "Pull the plug soldier!"

"What if we only turn half of them off, or at least keep the tree lit in the rec-room?" Steve King asked, kneeling beside the outlet, light cord in his hands. He also knew what it meant to the children, to all of them. They weren't just lights on a tree, they were shining, twinkling little lights of hope.

"Questioning my orders! I could have your strips for that Sergeant, is that what you want?"

"No Sir! It's just that—"

"Enough! Pull the plug, or spend the rest of our time here in a cell, you got that Sergeant!"

"Yes Sir…" Steve King said as he reluctantly, and against his better judgment gave the thin cord a tug from the outlet, and the tree went dark. He stood up beside the tree, but his head hung low, and he did not want to make eye contact with anyone, especially the girls. He felt as if he had let them down, and hated himself for it. Over their time spent together he had started to feel more like a grandfather to Kristen and Carmen, but now he felt as if he had betrayed them, and that he could not bear.

As Steve King started to walk passed the girls to leave the room, Kristen reached out to him, took hold of his arm, stopping him.

"It's okay Steve, it's not your fault." Kristen said softly, her sweet voice caressed his ears and sparked and idea.

"You two meet me by the elevators in ten minutes." He whispered, then walked on his way as if nothing was said.

Both girls stood silent until the Major and the other soldiers left the room. With the coast clear, Carmen quickly turned to Kristen and asked her what the Sergeant had said to her. Kristen answered her friend just as quickly, and they too exited the room and hurried to Kristen's quarters.

"Why would he want us to meet him there?" Carmen ask the second the door was closed behind them, knowing that no one else could hear.

"I have know idea, but I'm going to be there. If Steve has something in mind it has to be good."

"Maybe you two have just been working too close together… and he has a crush on you."

"What! That's stupid Car, he's in his sixties. What's wrong with you?"

"It was just a joke, damn."

"Well it wasn't funny." But now that idea had been put in Kristen's mind, and clouded her judgment. *What if she's right?* Kristen thought, *What will I do then?*

Kristen tried her best to push the thought from her mind and got ready to meet with Steve at the elevators, as did Carmen. A few minutes later they were standing in the dark shadows that engulfed the elevators, another of Major Harrisons ideas, cutting the power to all overhead lights in areas not readily used. They stood silent, huddled together, and feeling a little sheepish as they waited. Carmen kept checking her watch, then would glance down the corridor for movement.

"When did he say to meet him?" Carmen asked, checking her watch for the fifth time since they had arrived.

"He just said ten minutes, now hush, before someone hears you."

"Hears me? Who is going to hear me, there's no one here, no one but us. Besides it's a little creepy here."

"I know…" Kristen whispered. "I also know that the soldiers patrol this corridor every hour, so be quiet."

"Fine…"

But that quiet was suddenly interrupted by the two girls releasing a short, yet high pitched scream when a hand reached out of the darkness from behind them, and touched their arms that were locked together. "Shhhh…" Sergeant King breathed, his index finger touched to his cracked lips. "Follow me."

Steve King turn to face the elevator behind him, he inserted a key in the panel to the right of the door, and the door hissed as it slid open. He stepped inside and motioned for the girls to follow.

"Where are we going?" Carmen asked, as Kristen stepped inside, leaving her alone in the dark hallway.

"Down…" Was his only answer.

"I don't know…" Carmen shuffled her feet on the concrete floor.

"I'm going… with or without you." Kristen stated, slipping her arm around Steve's at his side.

"Fine…" Carmen gushed, stepping inside just as the door started to shut.

The three of them rode the elevator down, not saying a word until it came to rest at the very bottom of the shaft, and the doors opened. The three of them stepped out into a large area, with steel beams visible at the high ceiling, and huge machines stretched out in a line in front of them. Ten to twenty black barrels sat in front of each machine, in two sets of five, stacked, on each side of a walkway leading to the control panel of the machine.

"These are the generators for the building, girls."

"Wow, I never expected them to be so big." Kristen said in awe of their massive size.

"Well it takes a lot to keep a building the size of this one going." Steve led the girls down the isle in front of the generators. "The barrels are full of diesel fuel, that is what the generators run on. Each fifty gallon barrel will supply twenty hours of run time, per generator."

"That's all, twenty hours?" Carmen asked, surprised.

"Yes, so you see the Major does have his reasons. The main power grid of the city is shutting down. There is no one left out there to keep it running, and it is designed to shut down grid by grid if not manned. The entire city will be shut down in a few weeks, and these generators will then be our only source of power."

"I still don't see what the big deal is, when that happens we just cut back on electric use, right?" Carmen asked.

"That is true, to a point. The problem is that the entire shelter runs on electric, not just the lights, and stoves, but everything, the shutter doors that lead outside, the climate control, even the air that we breath down here."

"So what you are saying is that if there is no more electric, the doors can't be opened, and we will have no air?"

"Exactly, we all die down here."

"Oh shit…" Carmen spun around and took Kristen into her arms, hugging her. "I don't want to die down here, in the dark."

"Easy… that is a ways off, and we are working the problem out, but for now the only solution is to conserve energy, and bring in as much fuel as we can."

"Bring in fuel? You mean soldiers are going out and getting fuel?"

"Yes… we have been for over a month."

"So it is safe outside?"

"Far from it. We have lost several lives, and even more over the last couple weeks. Something seems to be stirring up the freaks, making it more difficult for us to find and retrieve fuel."

"What could have them stirred up?" Kristen asked, and suddenly remembered her dream. "Could there be people out there, could that be what's doing it?"

"I believe so, but the Major will not send out extra scouting parties, it's too dangerous."

"So what has all of this to do with us?" Carmen finally asked the important question.

"Well…" Steve gave a little, short lived chuckle.

"When I saw your faces, and those of the children when we killed the tree lights, I thought of something."

"What?" Kristen asked, her mood turning back around to a positive one.

"You see, the Major is closely monitoring the power usage, so when you plugged all the lights in it showed a spike, but I know there is a generator down here that is off the main building grid, energy pulled through it won't show on the monitor."

"So you are saying we can fire the trees back up?" Kristen was starting to bubble with excitement.

"No, just the one in the rec-room, and maybe the one outside…"

"Outside?" Kristen questioned, wondering what he was talking about, then the image flashed in her mind, the photo of the giant tree of lights atop the building. "You mean?"

"Yep… We can power it up from down here, it has always been supplied by that generator, I just had not thought about it until today."

"But what about the Major?"

"Like I said the power usage won't show on his monitors, and he very rarely ever goes to the rec-room. None of the soldiers are going to say anything, they didn't won't it shut down to begin with."

"I get that, but a seventy foot high tree of lights is going to be hard to hide." Carmen stated, hoping that Steve had an answer to that problem too.

"To conserve power we are only running thermal scans out side, and at ground level, he will never know."

"You are risking a lot for us." Kristen sighed, giving

the Sergeant a hug.

“Well it’s not just for you, if we light the tree outside, any survivors within twenty miles will be able to see the tree, or at least the star on top of it.”

“They can follow the star to us…” Kristen said just above a whisper, remembering her dream, and the star that the people in it were following. She had wrote it off, just a Christmas story entwined with her dream, but now she thought better, it was a sign.

“Exactly… But I can’t do this by myself, I’m gonna need both of your help to pull it off.”

“Just tell us what to do.” Kristen chimed, eager to get started.

It took the three of them four hours to get everything ready, filling the generator was the most difficult. Neither girl weighed more than a hundred pounds and the barrels were extremely heavy, but they worked it out. Running the lines and connecting them to the rec-room was much easier, though it held it’s own set of problems. Like the fear of electrocution that Carmen harbored that even she didn’t know about. But with hard work, and the suppression of personal fears they had done it, and it was the moment of truth. Time to flip the switch.

It was a large lever really, about a foot long, and the three of them stood before it, ready.

“Kristen, you want the honors?” Steve asked, wiping the black grease, and sweat from his brow.

“No, I think you should do it.”

“Okay then…” Steve reached up to the lever, clutched it firmly in his hand, and pulled it down with a grunt. “Damn thing was stiffer than I thought.”

The generator roared to life, there was a few sparks, and crackles were the lines connected, then the machine smoothed out into a steady hum.

"How we will know if it worked?" Kristen asked.

"We'll go plug the tree back in."

"No, outside, how will we know if we can't see out."

"Oh we will see out, come on." Steve quickly led the girls to the back of the room, to another elevator. He pushed the button and the doors slowly opened. This elevator was not like the other, it was dirty, grease on the handrail, dust on the floor and walls, a complete mess. "I took the liberty of hooking the freight elevator up to. Shall we go check on that tree?"

"Oh yes…" Kristen was boiling over, not only was she going to see the beautiful tree lit up high above the building, but she was going to get to see the outside world again.

"I don't know…is it safe?" Carmen questioned, not nearly as eager as Kristen.

"We're not going outside, Carmen… just to the ground level."

"How do we know there aren't any freaks on the ground level?"

"There aren't, not inside the building anyway, it is well secured."

"Forgive me Sergeant, but I've heard that before, back in sector 2 right before is was over ran."

"Christ Carmen, I was there too, this is different, this building was designed to keep people out." Kristen coaxed.

"So was sector 2, it was a prison, remember."

"Yeah, and it was to keep people in, not out."

"Carmen, you don't have to go, you can wait for us here." Steve assured her.

"I don't want to do that either, if you are attacked the freaks will be down here next."

"If that was to happen, you wouldn't have anyplace to go anyway."

"Good point, guess I'm coming too." Carmen joined them in the elevator, and they rode it up to the top.

Just to be safe, Sergeant King drew his sidearm as the elevator slowed to a stop, ready to fire when the door opened if need be. The door slid open and they were all staring at an empty utility room. It was dark since the power had been turned off to the ground levels. Steve withdrew a flashlight from his belt and the three made their way around the ground floor carefully, and with as little noise as possible. When they neared a pair of double doors with a sign that read Cafeteria over top them, Steve moved next to it, and put his hand on the door.

It was cold, no heat, and the girls were shivering. They had not dressed for cold weather, it was a constant sixty degrees in the underground shelter, and none of them had thought about the difference in temperature before they got on the elevator. It was cold enough to see their breath as they breathed, and the cloud formed around them quickly as their excitement, and fear grew standing outside the cafeteria doors.

"We should be able to see it from here, if it is on." Steve told them, then pushed the one door open. He stepped just inside, his light and pistol leading the way.

"It's clear…"

The two girls stepped in and when the glow of the white lights reflected off the snow and onto their chilled skin, they suddenly became warm, a warmth that filled them from the inside out.

"Oh my God…" Carmen sighed. "It's so beautiful.

"Even more pretty than the pictures," Kristen added as the girls stared out the large windows at the tree of lights and the giant star that rested atop it. "It's amazing."

"It sure is…" Steve too was awe struck as he stood behind the girls at the window. "Okay, it's on, now lets head back."

"So soon?" Kristen pleaded, she wasn't ready to give up her view of the outside world, even if she was freezing.

Carmen shivered, wrapping her arm around Kristen's waist, snuggling to her, feeling the slight warmth of their two bodies touching. She checked her watch, smiled, looked into Kristen's eyes, and said so happily: "Kristen it's twelve thirty… it's Christmas…"

Kristen smiled back at her, then to Steve. He also returned it to her, and at that moment Kristen spotted a flash in the corner of her eye. A bright sudden flash, much like that of gun fire at night. She turned to follow the flash outside the window, there was another flash, and a second later the glass of the window next to her cracked, much like a small spider web, with a small circular indent in the center.

"Down!" Sergeant King shouted, pushing the girls too the floor and away from the window. Carmen screamed, scared, though she did not know why for sure.

"What the hell?" Kristen shouted as soon as she hit the floor.

"Gun fire Kristen, that was a bullet that hit the glass. We have to get back down below, quick. Another hit like that could weaken the glass enough for the freaks to bust through."

"But where did the shot come from?"

Steve guided Kristen back up to the window on their knees, just high enough for them to be able to see the three trucks rolling in from the street. There were a mob of freaks chasing after them, twenty or thirty. Along the trucks people ran, weapons firing, most of them were soldiers, but some look like civilians. Kristen watched as they came closer and closer to the building. There were two people out in front taking out any freaks that happen to try and cut them off. At the back of the trucks were two more, holding off the mob that followed them.

"Only two… two to hold off all of those freaks? Is that even possible?" Kristen asked aloud, though it was more to herself.

"Seems to be working so far." Steve answered.

"I'm not looking, I just want to go back down now please." Carmen cried, begged.

"She's right, we have to get back down, now."

Kristen didn't move, she watched the small group fight for their lives, the soldiers were climbing up onto the trucks sides, and hoods, and the trucks were picking up speed, slowly leaving the civilians behind. The one man that had been at the rear with a soldier, dropped to his one knee, fired off what must have been a full clip into the mob, but they just kept coming. Kristen had seen that happen before, the freaks dropped dead, and the ones behind them just walked over them like they weren't even there. There was no loyalty, no love amongst the freaks. Just a constant hunger, and rage.

"Oh my god…" Kristen gasped. "It can't be…"

"What Kristen, what can't be?" Carmen asked, still laying on the floor, not about to even glance out of the window.

"I think it's her… the woman from my dream."

"Impossible…"

"What dream?" Steve asked, confused, staring out the window. "How can you even tell any of them are a woman from here."

"Because I've seen her before… Lets go, we have to get to them."

"This way… quickly." Steve lead them toward the main elevators, passed them and down a narrow hallway, and into a parking garage. They no longer than entered when the metal shutters started to lift. "Down, get down." He motion them behind the half wall of block between them and the half open shutter. They could now hear the gunfire, the engines roaring, and the howls of the infected. Carmen curled up on the floor behind the half wall, while Kristen kneeled to see over the wall, and Sergeant King aimed his pistol toward the opening metal door.

The first truck rolled in before the door was completely open, but just high enough for the truck to fit under it. By the time the second truck rolled in the soldiers had jumped off the first truck and had taken positions at the door. Two, one on each side of the open door, and the third at the large button that closed the door. The second truck rolled quickly across the garage and parked next to the first. The soldiers that rode on the hood of the second truck took up positions behind the two trucks.

Just ahead of the third and final truck two people in heavy coats ran through the door, then the third truck rolled in and passed them. By the time the third truck rolled to a stop in line with the first two the shutters had started to close. A soldier ran under them, along with three more people in shabby heavy coats. As the shutters closed down to the floor, two more people rolled under the shutters. The second the shutters connected with the concrete floor, the infected started slamming against them, bowing them inward, sounding like a thunderstorm was happening inside the garage.

Carmen cupped her hands over her ears and started screaming for them to stop. Kristen quickly stretched over her friend, trying to quiet her down, but Carmen was beyond scared, and with all they had already been through Kristen could not blame her. She too was afraid, but the curiosity of the people being so similar to those in her dream was to strong for her to ignore.

“Who the hell turn on that God-damned freak beacon out there?” Major Harrison shouted as he tossed his helmet to the garage floor. “Stupid, stupid… someone is going to pay for this.”

“It was my fault Sir.” Kristen said, stepping out from behind the half wall around Sergeant King.

“What, wha, what are you even doing up here?” He quickly spun and darted across the space between them until he was no more than two feet from her. “What the hell do you mean, your fault?”

"I…"

"I'm responsible Sir." Sergeant King said, stepping to Kristen's side.

"You're responsible for her being up here, Sergeant?"

"Yes Sir, and for the outside lights."

"I should shoot you here and now… you could have gotten us all killed."

"I wouldn't go that far Major, after all if it weren't for that shining star we wouldn't be here at all." A man said, stepping up behind the Major. A hood covered his head, and scarf was wrapped around the lower portion of his face, the only thing visible was his cool blue eyes. But his voice, his voice somehow seemed familiar to Kristen, familiar enough that she stepped forward, toward the man.

Steve reached out to stop her, but he was too late, she was just passed his grip. Kristen stepped passed the side of the Major as he watched her with his familiar stern glare. The man stood silent, staring at her, then without a single visible movement the man said through his scarf, one single word in pure disbelief: "Kristen?"

Kristen stopped at the sound of her name coming from the man, frozen, her body in complete shut-down. She stood staring at him as he leaned his head forward, removed his scarf and hood, then looked back up to her.

"Alex?"

Visit the official J.E. Steinman Website
For news, books, stories, and merchandise

www.wordsofrage.weebly.com

J.E. Steinman Books Published By Lulu Press

Solitude and Circumstance

Rage

Christmas Rages On

www.ingramcontent.com/pod-product-compliance
Ingram Content Group UK Ltd.
Pitfield, Milton Keynes, MK11 3LW, UK
UKHW041904190726
13854UKWH00003B/1080

9 781257 096176